WORDS TO READ

Carol Watson
Illustrated by Colin King

Series Editor: Heather Amery

Consultant: Betty Root
Centre for the Teaching of Reading
University of Reading

This is our house.

bird

nest

chimney

tree

roof

owl

cat

window

garage

flower

door

pram

wheelbarrow

dog

sack

2

It has

a very tall chimney,

a bright red roof,

five windows

and a big green door.

3

In the kitchen

saucers

cups

door

cakes

apron

bowl

glass

knife

table

fork

spoon

stool

chair

window

blind

clock

cooker

cupboard

saucepan

sink

tray

plate

bin

dustpan

brush

dog

5

The dog chases the cat

across the sink,

under the cooker,

over the table

and round the bin.

They knock down

cups and saucers,

a big saucepan,

a plate of cakes

and the red apron.

The men have come to paint the living room.

clock

mirror

picture

curtain

television

cushion

ladder

chair

rug

table

can

dog

paintbrush

We take down

the three pictures,

the orange curtains,

the old mirror

and the dusty clock.

They carry out

the small table,

a big chair,

the television

and the rug.

The men have finished.

clock

mirror

plant

television

lamp

cat

wool

chair

baby

ball

bricks

Dad keeps his car in the garage.

We help him to

wash the bonnet,   polish the lights,

clean the windscreen and the wheels.

The garden

tree

nest

leaf

fly

plant

brush

wall

pram

rake

butterfly

worm

seeds

spade

bird

watering can

bee

flower

treehouse

owl

door

step

bush

path

clothes peg

rubbish

grass

rope ladder

wheelbarrow

basket

bone

15

In the garden Dad likes to

dig the ground,

plant the seeds,

water the flowers

and sweep up the leaves

We play in the garden.

We chase butterflies,

pick up worms,

hide in the bushes

and climb the trees.

It is bathtime.

bubbles

sponge

cupboard

brush

tooth paste

tooth brush

tap

washbasin

bath

tooth paste

bathmat

towel

toilet

water

soap

18

In the bath

we turn on the taps,

splash the water,

make some bubbles

and play with the soap.

19

Bedtime

light

wardrobe

dress

drawer

jum[p]

dressing gown

slipper

jeans

boots

shoe

dog

cap

sock

hairbrush

curtain

clock

doll

lamp

book

pillow

pyjamas

nightdress

sheet

teddy

bed

comb

comic

bricks

21

At bedtime

we take off our shoes

and socks,

look for a hairbrush

and find a comb.

Dad puts us to bed.

He reads a book to us,

draws the curtains and kisses us goodnight.

23

Here is a puzzle.

Can you find mum, dad, baby, the cat,
two worms and a spotty dog?

THE SHOP

Carol Watson
Illustrated by Colin King

Series Editor: Heather Amery
Consultant: Betty Root

We go to the shop.

blind

window

jars

cake

shopkeeper

bag

bottles

basket

newspaper stand

pram

dog

t has

two big windows,

a striped blind,

a newspaper stand

and a shopkeeper.

Inside the shop.

shelf

window

scales

shopkeeper

knife

counter

cashier

till

cash desk

trolley

BREAD AND CAKES

cake

tin

bottle

bread

basket

packets

box

freezer

barrel

tube

29

Mum wants

a wire basket

and a big trolley.

We look at bottles

and tins.

We take

a box off the shelf,

peas from the freezer,

apples from the barrel

and a packet of sugar.

We look at the meat and fish.

MEAT and FISH

sausages

ham

fish

knife

paper

chicken

chops

bacon

We buy

five chops,

two big fish,

some sausages

and a fat chicken.

Mum buys vegetables and fruit.

VEGETABLES AND

onions

cauliflower

grapes

lemons

cabbages

cucumber

pineapples

lettuces

tomatoes

grapefruit

apples

orange

FRUIT

peaches

mushrooms

plant

pumpkin

scales

potatoes

carrots

melon

bananas

35

We pick up

a bunch of bananas,

a box of mushrooms,

a string of onions

and two lettuces.

The man weighs

some apples

and lots of carrots.

He drops a cabbage

and steps on a tomato.

We find the bread and cakes.

BREAD AND CAKES

icing

fruit cake

cake

chocolate cake

buns

loaf

doughnuts

bread

biscuit

bun

38

We take ten buns,

two loaves of bread,

a packet of biscuits

and a chocolate cake.

We stop at the dairy counter

DAIRY FOODS

milk

margarine

butter

cheese

cream

yoghurt

eggs

We buy

six pots of yoghurt,

two boxes of eggs,

three cartons of milk

and some cheese.

We find lots of things to read.

Mum stops to talk to her friends.

till

cashier

purse

bag

ice lolly

chocolate

freezer

box

43

We want

some new pencils,

coloured pens

and some sweets and chocolate for Dad.

At last we have finished.

Mum opens her purse and drops all her money.

We pay the cashier,

fill up the bags
and off we go.

Here is a puzzle.
Mum put these things into her bag.

cake

carrots

bananas

chicken

fish

cheese

eggs

sausages

lettuce

Can you see what she lost on the way home?

Here is another puzzle

Can you find a bottle, a jar, a cake, some bread and a string of onions?

THE TOWN

The Family goes to the town

This is our town.

church

roof

flag

park

flats

hotel

shops

lamp post

bus stop

garage

pavement

lorry

taxi

policeman

traffic lights

motor cycle

bicycle

police car

car

50

We go to town in the car.

hospital

factory

school

ambulance

road

offices

bus

drill

crossing

postman

The town has

a big hotel,

a block of flats,

a biscuit factory

and lots of shops.

Grandad is riding his bicycle. He goes past

a red van,

a big lorry,

a yellow taxi

and the school bus.

We stop at the garage.

light

van

car

spanner

battery

air
pump

petrol
pump

windscreen

bonnet

cloth

petrol
cap

bumper

tyre

water

bucket

oil

We help the man to put

petrol in the tank,

oil in the engine,

water in the radiator

and air in the tyres.

It is Daisy's first day at school.

clock

picture

brushes

paper

ruler

door

bookcase

book

card

rubber

pencil

crayon

glue

paint

paintbrush

scissors

The teacher says hello.

blackboard

$2 + 3 =$

window

chalks

jar

pen

register

notebook

map

cupboard

drawing pins

table

weight

scales

wastepaper bin

chair

The children are working hard.

They write with pencils,

paint pictures,

look at books

and cut up card.

When the teacher is not looking,

Daisy spills the paint,   squeezes the glue,

climbs on the bookcase   and tears up paper.

The workmen dig a hole in the ground.

brush
cement mixer
digger
cement
rail
motor
plank
bricks
drill
trowel
tap
shovel
barrel
earth
hosepipe
lamp
pipe
cat
boot

They are putting in new pipes. One man

trips over a shovel,

falls in the cement,

knocks over the drill

and breaks a pipe.

We go to the hospital to see Granny.

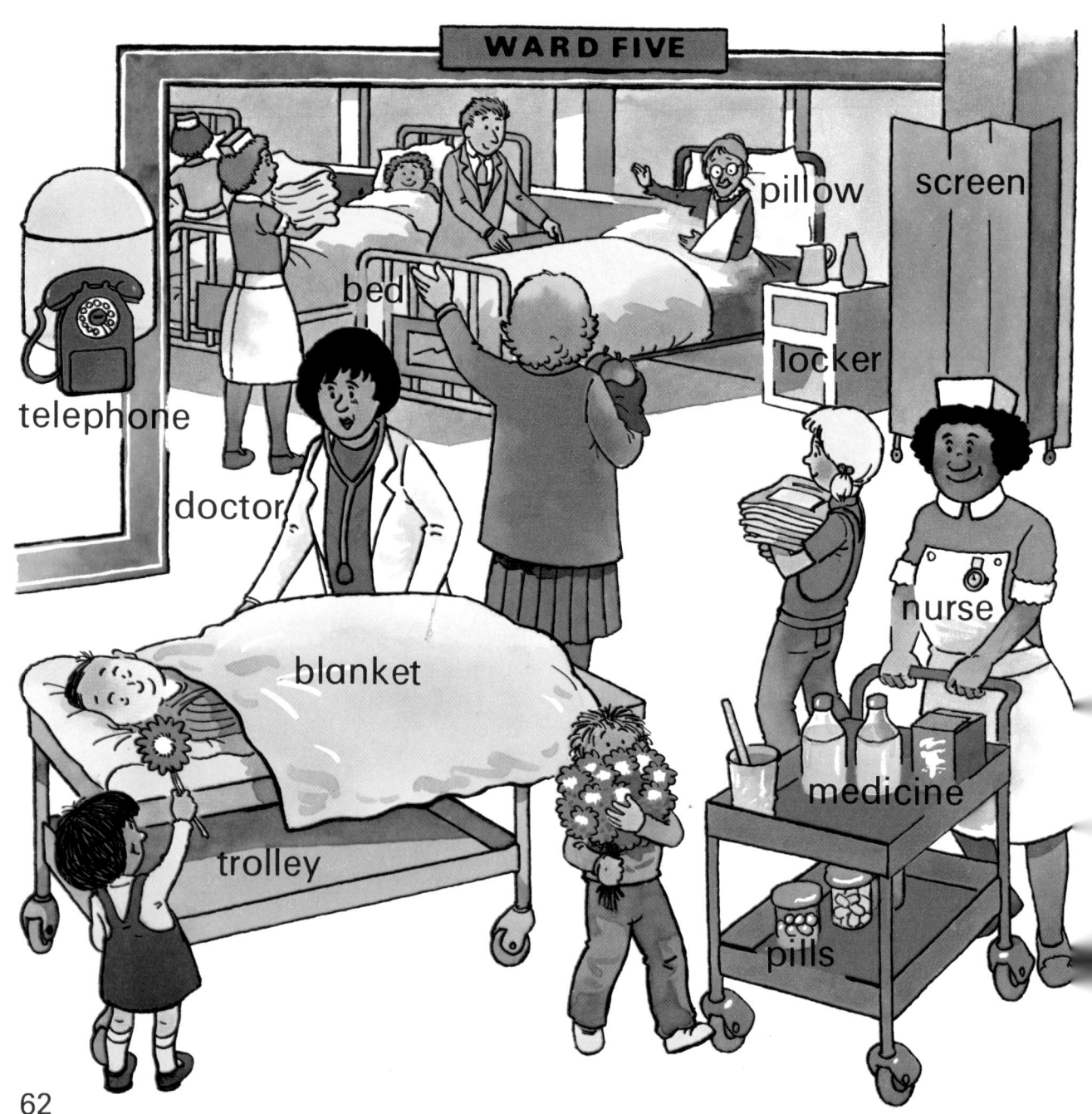

WARD FIVE

pillow

screen

telephone

bed

locker

doctor

blanket

nurse

trolley

medicine

pills

The nurses are very busy.

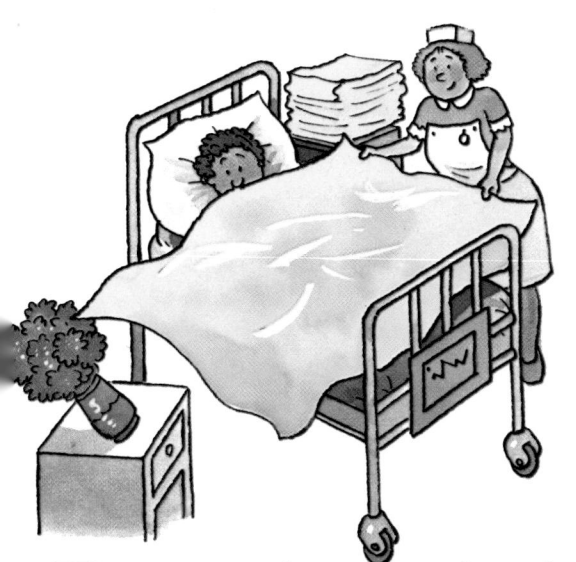

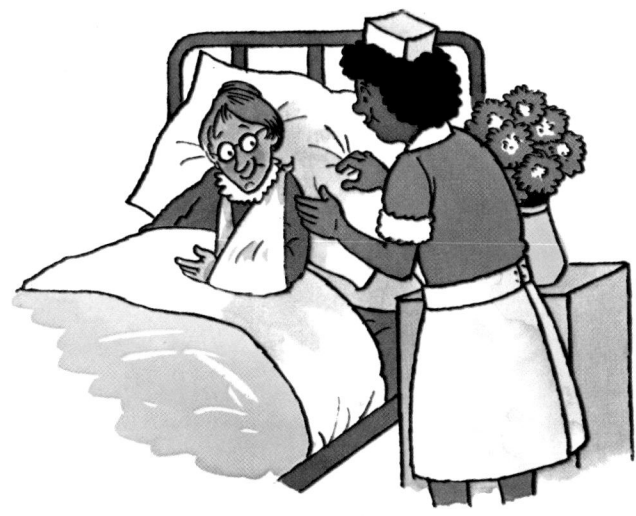

They make the beds,   straighten the pillows

and give the patients pills and medicine.

Sometimes we go to the swimming pool.

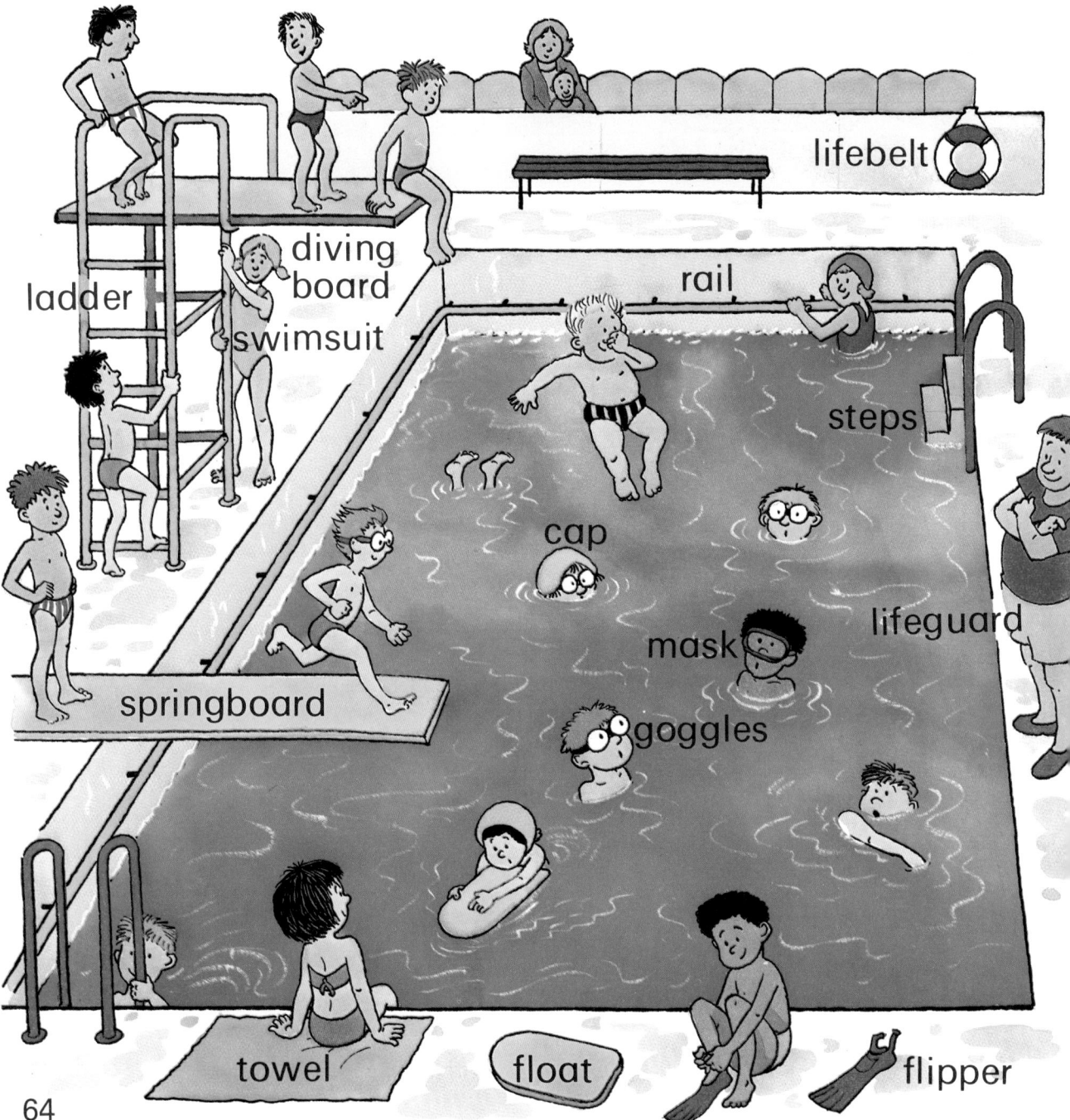

lifebelt

rail

ladder

diving board

swimsuit

steps

cap

lifeguard

mask

goggles

springboard

towel

float

flipper

There are lots of people in the water.

A boy climbs the ladder and dives off the board.

Daisy wears a cap   and swims with a float.

We go to the park to play.

kite

tree

slide

swings

grass

ball

path

bush

fence

gate

leaves

bench

pushchair

boat

ducks

lead

pond

flowers

The wind blows

a kite up in the sky,

the leaves off a tree

and the little boat across the pond.

We go to the railway station.

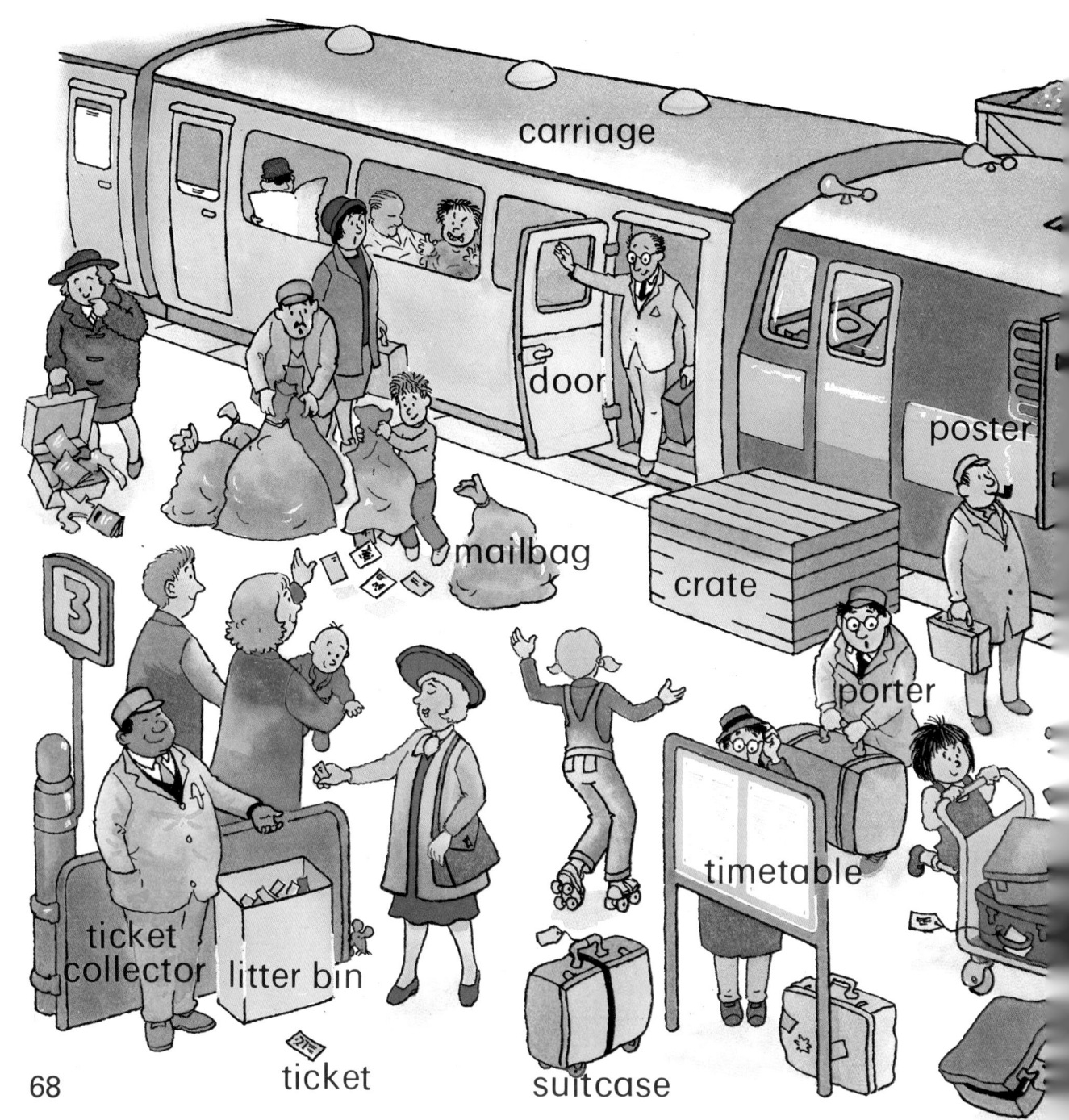

carriage

door

poster

mailbag

crate

porter

timetable

ticket collector

litter bin

ticket

suitcase

We are meeting Uncle Alf.

coal

clock

wagon

engine

driver

guard

signals

whistle

buffer

trolley

parcel

railway line

69

Uncle Alf gets out of the train,

puts down his suitcase,   calls for a porter,

trips over a mailbag   and hands in his ticket

The train is ready to leave the station.

The signal goes green. The guard closes a door,

looks at the clock   and blows his whistle.

Here is a puzzle.

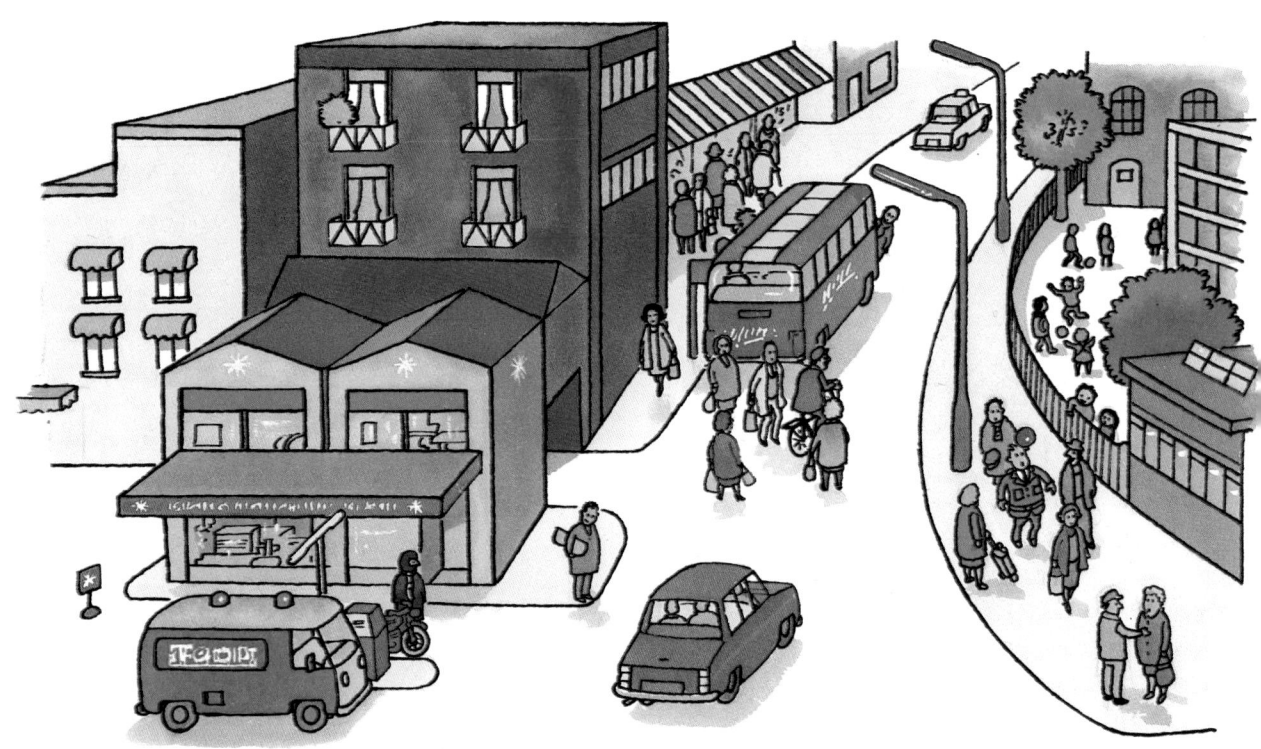

Can you find the policeman, the motorcycle, a petrol pump, a bicycle and a taxi?

First published in 1980
by Usborne Publishing Ltd
20 Garrick Street
London WC2 9BJ, England
© Usborne Publishing Ltd 1980

Printed in Belgium

The name Usborne and the device are
Trade Marks of Usborne Publishing Ltd.